Henry Climbs a Mountain

❧ *For Linda* ❧

www.houghtonmifflinbooks.com

The text of this book is set in ITC Garamond Book Condensed.
The illustrations are colored pencil and paint on paper.

Library of Congress Cataloging-in-Publication Data

Johnson, D. B. (Donald B.), 1944–
Henry climbs a mountain / written and illustrated by D.B. Johnson.
p. cm.
Summary: Although he loves his freedom, Henry goes to jail rather than
go against his principles. Based on the life of Henry David Thoreau.
ISBN 0-618-26902-9
1. Thoreau, Henry David, 1817–1862—Juvenile fiction. [1. Thoreau, Henry David,
1817–1862—Fiction.] I. Title.
PZ7.J6316355 Hde 2003
[E]—dc21
2002151172

Manufactured in the United States of America
WOZ 10 9 8 7 6 5 4 3 2 1

❖ Henry Climbs a Mountain ❖

D. B. Johnson

HOUGHTON MIFFLIN COMPANY

BOSTON 2003

Henry wanted to climb a mountain. But he had only one shoe.

His other shoe was at the shoemaker's being fixed. *I'll get it on my way,* he thought.

But on his way to the shoemaker's shop, Henry was stopped by Sam, the tax collector.
"Henry," he said, "you haven't paid your taxes."
"Pay a state that lets farmers own slaves? Never!" said Henry.

"You'll have to pay or go to jail," Sam said.
"Then take me to jail!" said Henry. And Sam did.

The door slammed shut. Henry lay down on the bed and looked up at the white walls and the white ceiling.

He put his bare foot against the wall. *I wish I had my other shoe,* Henry thought.

He took crayons from his pocket and drew a shoe on the white wall.

Beside the shoe, he drew a flower with a hummingbird on it.

Next, Henry drew the tree the hummingbird lived in.

Under the tree, he drew a path that crossed a river and climbed a mountain. Henry got his shoes wet.

As he drew up the wall, he sang a song: *The bear goes over the mountain, The bear goes over the mountain, The bear goes over the mountain, To see what he can see.*

Henry climbed up waterfalls. He marched in and out of clouds.

When it started to rain, Henry pulled his hat down and put on his coat.

He drew a hawk soaring in the clouds on the ceiling.

At the top of the mountain, Henry met a traveler coming up the other side.

He was singing this song: *The other side of the mountain, The other side of the mountain,*
The other side of the mountain, Will set me free at last.

Henry and the traveler sat together on the mountaintop. They talked and laughed and sang more songs.

"You have no shoes," said Henry. "Are you walking far?"
"As far as the star in the North," the traveler said.
"That's a long way," said Henry. "Take my shoes!"

The traveler put on Henry's shoes. He stood and waved. "Thank you, friend," he called.

Henry started back down the mountain.
The path went down and up and down again over sharp rocks that hurt his feet.

He tripped over tree roots and logs in the path. "Ouch!" said Henry.

Once, he caught his foot in a rabbit hole.

Henry rolled down the last hill and splashed across a river.

He had not slept all night. The sun was coming up when he stumbled into the small room.

Just then the door opened. It was Sam.

"Someone has paid your taxes, Henry," Sam said. "How does it feel to be free?"

Henry smiled. "It feels like being on top of a very tall mountain!" he said.

And he walked to the shoemaker's shop to buy a new pair of shoes.

❧ About Henry ❧

Henry David Thoreau was a great thinker and writer who lived in Concord, Massachusetts, more than 150 years ago. Henry loved to climb mountains: Katahdin in Maine, Monadnock in New Hampshire, and Greylock in Massachusetts. He loved being outdoors and being free to climb anytime he wanted. Nothing could stop Henry from roaming free. One time he spent a night locked in jail, but even then he did not feel shut in. He wrote: *"It was like traveling into a far country, such as I had never expected to behold, to lie there for one night."* ("Civil Disobedience").

Henry went to jail for not paying his taxes. He said he wouldn't pay taxes to a government that let some people buy and sell and own other people. This was slavery, and Henry hated it. He even helped slaves run away from their owners to be free in Canada.

Henry went to jail to be an example. He hoped others would also stop paying their taxes. If enough people went to jail, he thought, the leaders of the country would change the laws and end slavery forever. Henry told all this to the people of Concord in a speech called "Civil Disobedience." The speech became his most important writing and was read all over the world. Mahatma Gandhi used Henry's ideas to free the people of India from the British. In America, Martin Luther King Jr., who was also inspired by Henry's writings, went to jail many times to get the government to treat all people equally.

Even though Henry Thoreau was in jail for only one night, his ideas about how people can change bad laws without fighting are still being used today. This is what he wrote in his book *Walden:*

"One afternoon, near the end of the first summer, when I went to the village to get a shoe from the cobbler's, I was seized and put into jail, because I did not pay a tax to, or recognize the authority of, the state which buys and sells men, women, and children, like cattle at the door of its senate-house."